For the real Janet Grenzke and
and her partner, Don Kroodsma,
and of course, for Heidi.—J.Y.

For my bird boy.—A.W.

Text copyright © 2022 Jane Yolen
Illustration copyright © 2022 Anna Wilson

Book design by Melissa Nelson Greenberg

Published in 2022 by CAMERON + COMPANY, a division of ABRAMS.
All rights reserved. No portion of this book may be reproduced,
stored in a retrieval system, or transmitted in any form or by any
means, mechanical, electronic, photocopying, recording, or oth-
erwise, without written permission from the publisher.

Library of Congress Cataloging-in-Publication Data available.
ISBN: 978-1-951836-40-5

Printed in China

10 9 8 7 6 5 4 3 2 1

CAMERON KIDS is an imprint of CAMERON + COMPANY

CAMERON + COMPANY
Petaluma, California
www.cameronbooks.com

LOVE BirdS

by JANE YOLEN

illustrated by ANNA WILSON

cameron kids

Jon walked down the street quietly.
He knew no one in this new town.
Been there a month, he and his mom,
most of the summer gone,
and he hadn't talked to anyone his age.
"Honestly," his mom told a neighbor,
"you'd think he didn't know how to talk."
Jon's mom sure knew how to do that.

Jon walked silently past his mother's chatter,
past a boy throwing a ball against a garage door,
ka-thunk, ka-thunk, ka-thunk.

Past children laughing on swings.
Clink, swish, ha-ha!

He heard the growl of
Mrs. McGrath's lawn mower,

the swee-swish of
Mr. Lee's sprinklers,

and the loud chorus of music
as a car full of teens rolled past.

Jon may not have been talking,
but he sure was listening.
Mostly he listened to birds.
He listened to their dawn chorus
in the early morning:
bright cardinal with its piercing song,
Carolina wren caroling joyfully,

gulls in the fields shrieking after a tractor,

the tap, tap, tap of a woodpecker
at work on a tree.

He listened to birds in the afternoon:
crows conversing with dark caws,
chickadee calling its own name,
bubbly-voiced house wrens,
and the raucous cries of jays.

He listened to birds in the evening:
a single robin singing to a streetlight,
geese in long vees honking homeward,
barn swallows twittering clatter
as they headed to the roost,
and the lullaby coos of the local doves
sitting on their ready nests.
Jon always listened.

Especially for autumn owls.

One early evening,
in a small copse of trees behind his house,
Jon heard, "Who cooks for you?"
the song of the barred owl.
He began to call back, imitating its voice,
inviting it closer, and closer,
till the two of them were in a full duet.
The call came threading through the trees,
throaty and lovely.

And when another owl responded
from the nearest pines,
Jon saw its shadow leave the woods.
He moved toward it, a shadow himself.

COOKS FOR YOU
COOKS FOR YOU

Only it wasn't a bird.

It was a different listener,
a girl about his age.
They'd been calling back and forth
all that time, each one
hoping for an owl,
and finding one another.

Jon didn't have time for disappointment,
for the girl held out her hand.
"Janet," she said, "I thought you were a barred."
And then she laughed,
a sound bubbly as a wren's song.
"Not barred. Jon," he said.
He sounded as brassy as a jay.

Then Jon, who rarely talked,
and Janet, who always listened,
spent hours jabbering
with one another,
about nights and nightjars,
about nests and nestlings,
about hoots and calls,
about feathers and wings.

And still talking
and still listening,
they walked home together,
because—though they hadn't known it before—
they lived just around the block
from one another,
an owl's call away.
They promised to meet
the very next morning
to walk to school.

From then on,
when the sun rose
and the birds began to sing,
Jon and Janet added their own voices
to the dawn chorus.

For days and weeks,
and into the years,
they listened and talked,
till, for both of them, their voices
became the most important sound
in the whole wide world—
the voice of a best
and beloved friend.

AUTHOR'S NOTE

This book is a kind of partner to my book *Owl Moon*, which is about my daughter, Heidi, going owling with her father when she was very young. (He later did the same with her younger brothers.) But this story takes that child, a bit older, on a different trip—to one of friendship and love. This is not Heidi's real story, though she still is an ardent owler and leads the OMG (Owl Moon Gang) once a year on a midnight tour of the western Massachusetts woods to call down owls for the Audubon Christmas Bird Count.

This book is dedicated to Professor Don Kroodsma, my late husband's best friend and pioneer in birdsong recognition, who taught him not only how to recognize birdsong, but to record it. They took many trips together recording birds. And the book is also for Dr. Kroodsma's partner, my neighbor and longtime birding pal for all the Stemple birders, Janet Grenzke. The boy is named after her son, Jon. To read more about Dr. Kroodsma, go to: www.donaldkroodsma.com.